Please renew or return items by due date

www.hertfordshire.gov.uk/libraries

Renewals and enquiries: 0300 123 4049

Textphone for hearing or
speech impaired users: 01992 555 506

**There's a lot going on at Hertfordshire
Libraries! Scan the QR code to find out
more . . .**

23

Hertfordshire

KV-119 -144

D1523563

Max and Chaffy - Search for the Ice Chaffy! (Book 3)
is a
DAVID FICKLING BOOK

First published in Great Britain in 2023 by
David Fickling Books,
31 Beaumont Street,
Oxford, OX1 2NP

Text and illustrations © Fumboo Ltd, 2023
Colouring by Emily Kimbell, 2023

978-1-78845-263-2

1 3 5 7 9 10 8 6 4 2

The right of Jamie Smart to be identified as the author and illustrator
of this work has been asserted in accordance with the Copyright,
Designs and Patents Act 1988.

Papers used by David Fickling Books are from well-managed
forests and other responsible sources.

MIX
Paper from
responsible sources
FSC® C104723
FSC
www.fsc.org

DAVID FICKLING BOOKS Reg. No. 8340307

A CIP catalogue record for this book
is available from the British Library.

Printed and bound in China by Toppan Leefung

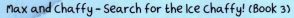

Max & Chaffy
on the
Search for the
Ice Chaffy!

d·b
FICKLING
David Fickling Books

A new day dawns on
Animal Island...

...but everything looks
a bit different...

3

...although someone hasn't noticed yet!

That's what we were **TRYING** to tell you, Max!

If you're going outside, you should wrap up warm!

Ziiiiip!

And now you're both ready to go!

Thank you!

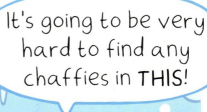

Doompf!

Crump!

19

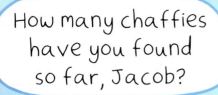

How many chaffies have you found so far, Jacob?

Umm . . .

None.

But when I **DO** find a chaffy, then I can wear the **OFFICIAL BADGE!**

I found a CHAFFY!

Special chaffy finder badge

21

23

Well, we've never found an **ICE CHAFFY** before!

But me and Chaffy are very good at finding things . . .

Meep!

. . . and I know some facts about chaffies that might help us!

Meep meep!

Let's see . . .

Does an Ice Chaffy have ONE-AND-A-HALF-EARS?

Fact one: eature has nd-a-half ears!

Yes!

Is an Ice Chaffy WHITE?

It's . . . ICE colour

Fact two: eature is white!

Does an Ice Chaffy like to eat LETTUCE?

Who DOESN'T?

Fact three: (last fact) eature likes lettuce!

Crumbles' vegetable patch!

29

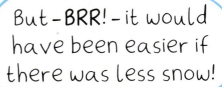

This is a great start!

But - **BRR!** - it would have been easier if there was less snow!

What you need is a **SHOVEL**. But I lent mine to **BRADLEY!**

Then we'll go and find Bradley next!

Have fun!

Bradley's Post Office!

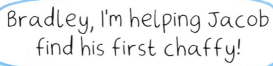

Bradley, I'm helping Jacob find his first chaffy!

And we need a shovel! Could we borrow that one?

Oh, I'm afraid I need it.

You see, earlier today I dropped my breakfast burrito in the snow . . .

Can you help Max find Chaffy?

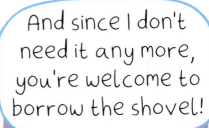

Police H.Q.

So, now we can't reach the telescope!

Well, you're in luck, because we have a **SHOVEL**!

I can **DIG** for your ladder!

51

I can see Mum and Dad by the lighthouse!

There might be an Ice Chaffy in the Ice Caverns!

Ooh, exciting!

Pheep pheep!

Deputy Constable Chaffy is right, it might be dark in the Ice Caverns!

Take this torch, so you can see where you're going!

The
Ice
Caverns!

Slip!

Oh no!

Jacob! Are you okay?

I'm fine! I'm not sure how I can get back out though.

69

The Mountain Top!

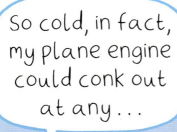

No. This is all my fault!

I forgot the most important rule of the Chaffy Finding Club!

IMPORTANT: Only ever look for chaffies where it is SAFE TO DO SO!

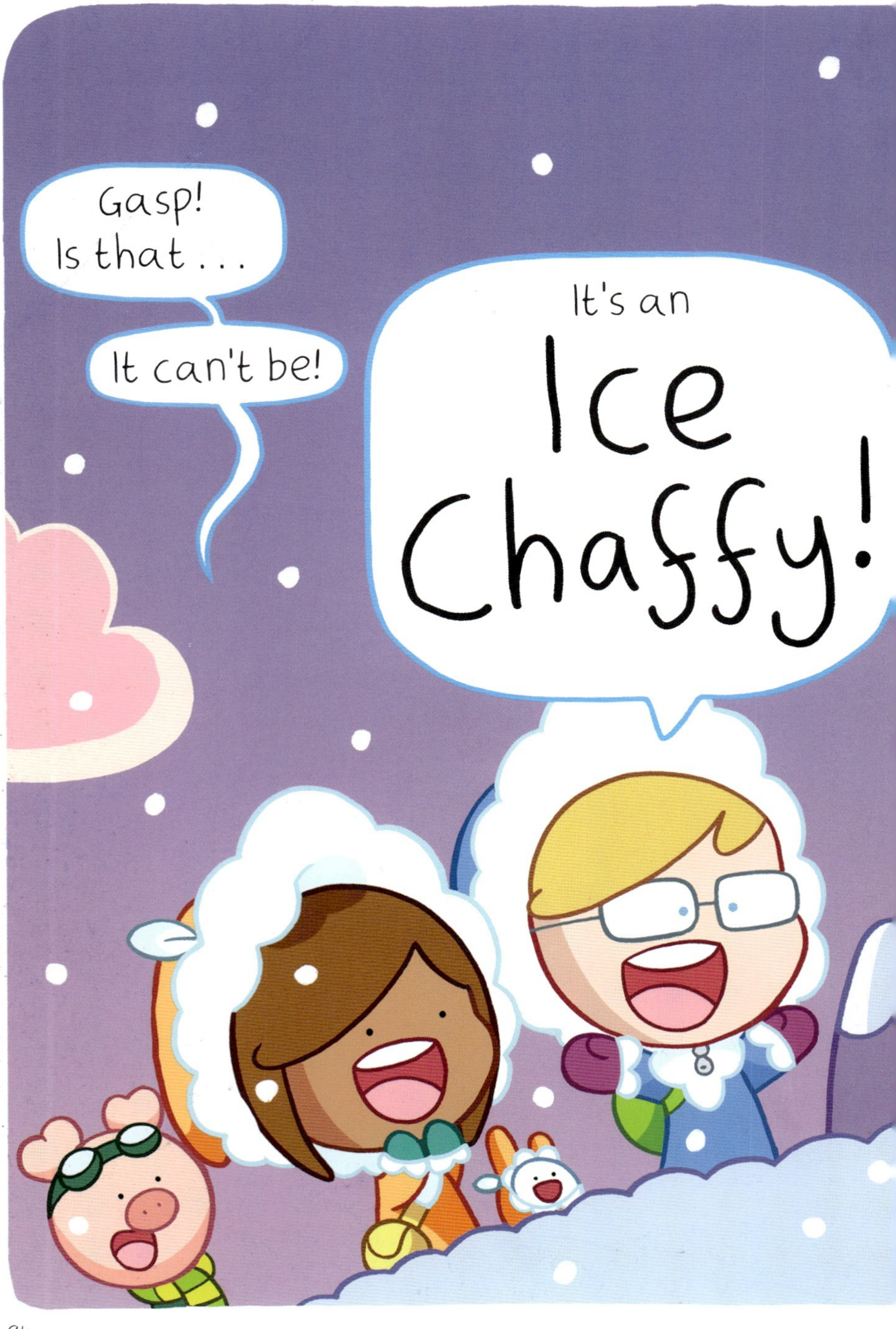
Gasp! Is that . . .
It can't be!
It's an Ice Chaffy!

The **ICE CHAFFY** is doing this!

It's growing an **ICE BRIDGE!**

Ice Chaffy has found us a way home!

105

It's going to take me ages to walk up the ice slide, I might just go home the long way.

I think I should go home too. Thank you for all your help, Max and Chaffy!

I'm going to look for a chaffy who belongs with me . . .

. . . and hopefully I'll find one somewhere a bit warmer! Haha!

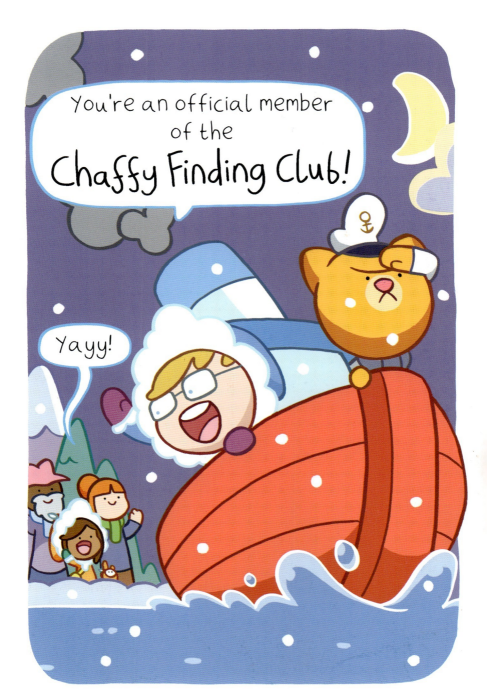

113

But wait!
The search isn't over! Deputy Constable Chaffy has spotted a lot of Animal Island's birds getting chilly in the snow. Can **YOU** help to round them up?

Crumbles' Vegetable Patch

Grey Bird

Green Bird

Pink Bird

Bradley's Post Office

Yellow Bird

Brown Bird

Purple Bird

Police H.Q.
Yellow Bird

Brown Bird

Grey Bird

The Ice Caverns
Yellow Bird

Blue Bird

Green Bird

The Mountain Top
Yellow Bird

Purple Bird

Blue Bird

Answers this way!

Answers

Well done! Now the birds are all toasty and warm with me! In case you missed any, here's where they all were.

Crumbles' Vegetable Patch

Grey Bird

Green Bird

Pink Bird

Bradley's Post Office

Yellow Bird

Brown Bird

Purple Bird

Police H.Q.

Yellow Bird

Brown Bird

Grey Bird

The Ice Caverns

Yellow Bird

Blue Bird

Green Bird

The Mountain Top

Yellow Bird

Purple Bird

Blue Bird

More adventures with

OUT NOW!

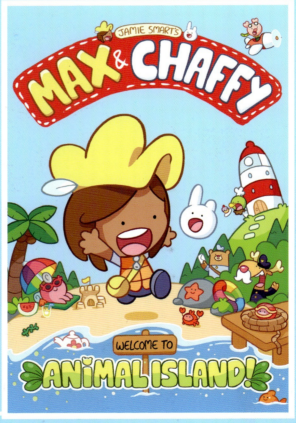

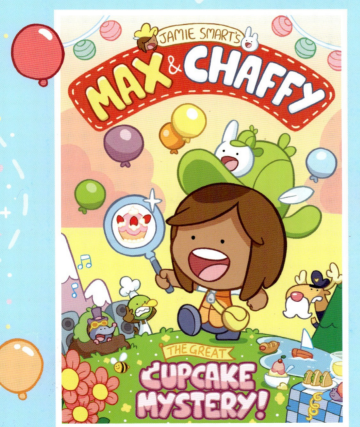

There's a whole world to explore...

FIND CHAFFY

www.findchaffy.com

Hi! I'm Jamie Smart.
I hope you loved reading about Max and Chaffy.
I really enjoyed writing and drawing it.
Thank you to my friends Emily, Rosie and Katie
who all helped me make this book too!
I've also created other books, like the best-selling

 and LOOSHKIN

Making up stories and looking for chaffies
are my two favourite things!